Hoppy & Joe

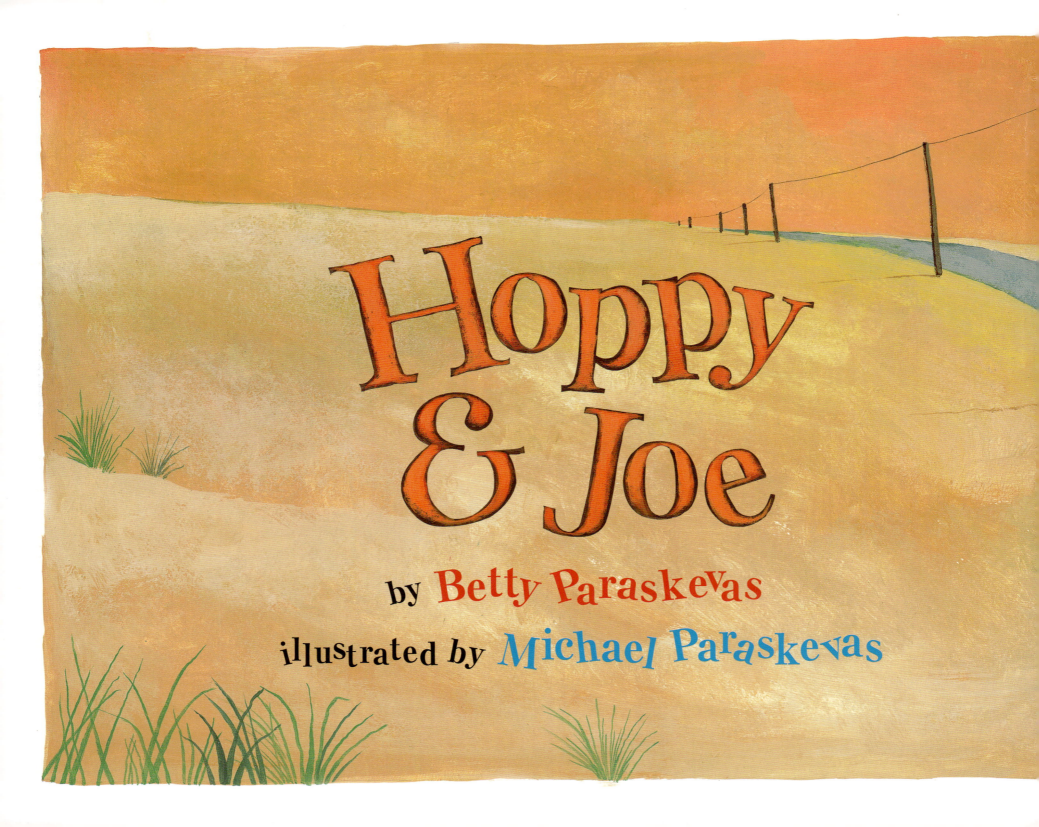

Hoppy & Joe

by Betty Paraskevas

illustrated by Michael Paraskevas

Simon & Schuster Books for Young Readers

On a narrow strip

of land between the ocean and the bay known as Sunshine Beach, there was a tiny stand with a big sign that read, GINO'S LEMON ICE.

This was Joe's world. Every morning, Joe would watch Gino squeeze the lemons and stack the pleated paper cups. He'd fix his eyes on Gino's face, tilt his head, first to one side and then to the other, and listen as Gino shared his thoughts.

But when the umbrella brigade began crossing the dunes, Gino got busy serving his customers and for the rest of the day, Joe would wander the beach alone.

Sometimes he'd sit near a family having fun, and pretend he was part of the group, hoping they'd toss him the ball or a snack, but eventually he'd grow weary and move on.

After a dip in the sea, Joe would shake himself dry, stretch out on the sand and wait for the long, lonely day to end.

One morning he walked to the end of the jetty and found a seagull stuck between two rocks. "What are you doin' there?" he asked.

"Tryin' to get out," the bird squawked.

Joe noticed that the gull had lost part of his leg struggling to get loose.

"Gee, I'm sorry about your leg," he murmured.

"Just get me outta here while I still have the other one," the gull demanded, turning his head so that Joe couldn't see the tears. But he didn't fool Joe one bit.

When Joe carried the wounded seagull inside the lemon-ice stand, Gino shouted, "You can't bring that bird inside, Joe. He'll drive away my customers. Take him out, right now."

Joe did as he was told and found a place for the gull behind the little stand, and Gino was more than a bit miffed by Joe's constant devotion to the bird.

"Hey, Joe," the gull would whimper, "see if you can find a paper plate with some ketchup left on it. I can't eat these fries without ketchup."

And sometimes he'd say, "Phew, it's so stuffy back here. I feel a teensy bit faint. How about a little ride, Joe? I just want to feel the wind in my feathers."

One day he told Joe of his dream to fly south. "I'm tellin' you, Joe, I was revved up and ready to go." Then he sighed. "I'll never make it now."

"Gee, I'm glad you're not going," Joe said. "I never had a friend before. Oh, there's Gino, but he's family, and he's busy all day."

"Yeah, well," said the gull, "I never had a dog before—for a friend, I mean," and Joe saw a fleeting twinkle in his eyes.

When the bruised and battered gull finally succeeded in hopping about, Joe shouted, "Go, Hoppy, go!"

Hoppy never went near the lemon-ice stand again and that was fine with Gino—good riddance. But from that day on Joe's world changed. Every morning he'd head down the beach to the snack bar, where he knew Hoppy would be waiting for him.

Summer was humming and the days flew by like the pages of a favorite book in a persistent breeze. Joe loved to run along the beach with Hoppy on his back, shouting, "Faster, Joe. Let's really kick up some sand."

Gino kept the stand open late every evening, and Hoppy and Joe liked to talk as they watched the moon spill diamonds on the sea. Hoppy would say, "I'm not kiddin' you, Joe. You'd love it down south. This old bird at the county dump told me they got palm trees, and sand that sparkles like sugar crystals, and water so clear you can see right to the bottom of the ocean."

And sometimes they didn't talk at all.

But the golden days on Sunshine Beach ended when a black cloud arrived in the form of a letter, advising Gino that he could no longer rent the stand because the land had been sold to a restaurant chain.

Gino sat for a long time with his face in his hands. Then he said, "Joe, we're moving south. At least we'll be able to stay open all year."

Joe rushed off to tell Hoppy. "Hoppy, Gino says we're movin' south."

"No kiddin', Joe! Well, in case I don't see you again, have a good trip."

Joe's eyes were huge circles. "Hoppy, you're the one who always talks about goin' south. This is our big chance!"

"Look, Joe! My long-distance flyin' days are over and my landin' gear ain't what it used to be."

"You can do it. Just follow the truck, Hoppy. I promise I'll be watchin' for you every minute."

"Sure, Joe. While you're in the truck with Gino, all comfy and cozy, I'll be up there all alone, beatin' my wings."

"Gee, I'm sorry. I wish you could ride in the truck but Gino would never agree to that."

"I can't make it, Joe."

"Think, Hoppy—you and me, just lying around, soakin' up all that sunshine."

"You don't understand, Joe. . . . I'm, I'm . . . scared."

"You? SCARED? Hoppy, I never met anyone as brave as you."

"Really?"

"Would I lie?"

"You really think I can make it?"

"I know you can!"

"Maybe you're right. Gosh, darn it, I gotta try. How much time do I have to get in shape?"

"We leave in a week."

Joe cheered Hoppy on as he
trained for the long flight, racing
through the sky, making circles
around the sun and practicing his
landing technique. And then came
the big day—they were ready to leave.

The old truck was making good time. Gino felt great. He'd made the right decision. It was just the two of them, following the sun. He smiled and looked at Joe hanging halfway out the window, his eyes on the sky.

They had gone about four hundred miles when Gino stopped for gas. Joe raced into the brush.

"Hoppy, *psst,* Hoppy, where are you?"

"I'm over here, Joe."

"Gee, Hoppy, you don't look so good."

"My wing is givin' me trouble."

"I don't want to leave you like this."

"I'll be okay. Better not keep Gino waitin'."

Hoppy saw the truck moving below him. There was good old Joe hanging out the window. "Hey, Joe! I'm up here, Joe." A blast of wind hit him head-on and a sharp pain surged through his wing. He was losing altitude, tumbling closer and closer to the ground. He managed to level off just in time. His whole body was weary with pain as he struggled to climb higher in the lonely sky. And Hoppy knew he wasn't going to make it.

Once again Gino pulled in for gas. He scratched his head as Joe disappeared into the woods. "Crazy dog," he mumbled.

Joe kept his nose to the ground until he found Hoppy. "Gee, Hoppy, you really look awful."

"Listen, Joe, I feel like a handful of loose feathers in a big paper bag. I'm all quivery and I need something to eat."

"You're gonna have to trust me," Joe said. "Get on my back." Hoppy, too weary to argue, did as he was told.

Gino was dumbstruck when he saw Joe approaching the truck. He thought he'd seen the last of that gull. "You crazy bird, get away." He began flapping his arms. Hoppy hung on.

"Joe, I'm not letting that bird in the truck. Now get in!"

Joe didn't flick so much as a whisker. He wasn't going to leave his only friend behind.

Gino was baffled. Joe had never disobeyed him before. "Get in the truck," he shouted, and he lifted the gull from Joe's back.

Joe planted his backside firmly on the road and stared at Gino. There was something in his eyes that made Gino stop.

Hoppy's frail little frame trembled in his grasp. This poor little guy was Joe's friend and he'd had more than his share of hard luck.

Gino cleared his throat and whispered, "It's okay. You're just tired, and no wonder! Eight hundred miles! And all on your own. I guess we can make room for Joe's best friend." One of Hoppy's tears escaped and splashed onto Gino's hand. "We'll have to get you something to eat. Oh, and I guess you should have a name! We'll call you Hoppy."

The old truck rolled along as Hoppy listened to Gino talk about his plans for their future. Those french fries really hit the spot. Joe was asleep beside him. Friends didn't come any better than good old Joe, and as they continued south along the highway, Hoppy was sure of one thing:

He was one lucky bird.

To Lisa Fann
Trevor Taylor
and Tayce Taylor

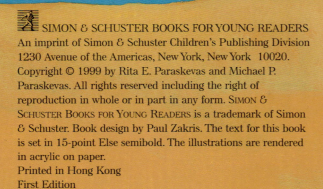

SIMON & SCHUSTER BOOKS FOR YOUNG READERS
An imprint of Simon & Schuster Children's Publishing Division
1230 Avenue of the Americas, New York, New York 10020.
Copyright © 1999 by Rita E. Paraskevas and Michael P.
Paraskevas. All rights reserved including the right of
reproduction in whole or in part in any form. SIMON &
SCHUSTER BOOKS FOR YOUNG READERS is a trademark of Simon
& Schuster. Book design by Paul Zakris. The text for this book
is set in 15-point Else semibold. The illustrations are rendered
in acrylic on paper.
Printed in Hong Kong
First Edition
10 9 8 7 6 5 4 3 2 1

LIBRARY OF CONGRESS CATALOGING-IN-PUBLICATION DATA
Paraskevas, Betty.
Hoppy and Joe / written by Betty Paraskevas ;
illustrated by Michael Paraskevas.
p.   cm.
Summary: A lonely dog befriends an injured seagull at
the beach, and together they find a way to go south.
[1. Gulls—Fiction. 2. Dogs—Fiction. 3. Friendship—
Fiction. 4. Beaches—Fiction.] I. Paraskevas, Michael,
1961–   ill. II. Title.
PZ7.P2135Ho   1999
[Fic]—dc21
97-48685